Enid Blyton's

MR STAMP-ABOUT
IN A FIX

and other stories

CLIVEDEN PRESS

Published in Great Britain in 1994 by Cliveden Press,
an imprint of Egmont Publishing Limited, Egmont House,
PO Box 111, Great Ducie Street, Manchester M60 3BL.
Printed in Finland

ISBN 0 7498 2040 3

Enid Blyton

Enid Blyton was born in London in 1897. Her childhood was spent in Beckenham, Kent, and as a child she began to write poems, stories and plays. She trained to be a teacher but she devoted her whole life to being a children's author. Her first book was a collection of poems for children, published in 1922. In 1926 she began to write a weekly magazine for children called *Sunny Stories*, and it was here that many of her most popular stories and characters first appeared. The magazine was immensely popular and in 1953 it became *The Enid Blyton Magazine*.

She wrote more than 600 books for children and many of her most popular series are still published all over the world. Her books have been translated into over 30 languages. Enid Blyton died in 1968.

Contents

Millicent Mary's surprise

Once there was a little girl called Millicent Mary. She had a dear little garden of her own, and in the early spring the very first things that came up were the white snowdrops.

Millicent Mary loved them. She loved the straight green stalks that came up, holding the white bud tightly wrapped up at the top. She liked the two green leaves that sprang up each side. She loved to see the bud slowly unwrap itself, and hang down like a little bell.

But she was always very disappointed because the white bells didn't ring.

"They ought to," said Millicent Mary, and she shook each snowdrop to see if she could make it ring. "Bells like this should ring – they really should! Ring, little snowdrop, ring!"

But not one would ring. Still, Millicent Mary wouldn't give it up. Every morning when she put on her hat and coat and went into the garden, she bent down and shook the snowdrops to see if perhaps today they would say ting-a-ling-a-ling. But they never did.

One day she went to her garden when the snow was on the ground. The snowdrops were buried beneath the snow, and Millicent Mary had to scrape the white snow away very gently to find out where her snowdrops were.

At last all the little white bells were showing. She shook them but no sound came. "Well, you might have rung just a tiny tune to tell me you were grateful to me for scraping the snow away!" said Millicent Mary.

She was just going to stand up and go to the shed to fetch her broom when she saw something rather strange. The snow on the bed nearby seemed to be moving itself – poking itself up as if something was underneath it, wriggling hard.

Millicent Mary was surprised. She was even more surprised when she heard a very tiny voice crying, "Help me! Oh, help me!"

"Goodness gracious!" said the little girl. "There's something buried under the snow just there – and it's got a little tiny voice that speaks!"

She began to scrape away the snow, and her soft, gentle fingers found something small and strange under the white blanket. She pulled out – well, guess what she pulled out!

Yes – you guessed right. It was a tiny pixie, a fairy with frozen silver wings and a little shivering body dressed in a cobweb dress.

"Oh, thank you!" said the pixie in a tiny voice, like a bird cheeping. "I was so tired last night that I crept under a dead leaf and fell asleep. And when I awoke this morning I found a great, thick, cold, white blanket all over me – and I couldn't get it off! Just wait till I catch the person who threw this big blanket all over the garden!"

Millicent Mary laughed. "It's snow!" she said. "It isn't a real blanket. You poor little thing, you feel so cold, you are freezing my fingers. I'm going to take you indoors and get you warm."

She tucked the pixie into her pocket and went indoors. She didn't think she would show the fairy to anyone, because she might vanish – and Millicent Mary didn't want her to do that. It was fun having a pixie, not as big as a doll, to warm before the fire!

The pixie sat on the fender and stretched out her frozen toes to the dancing flames. Millicent Mary took a piece of blue silk out of her mother's rag-bag and gave it to the pixie.

"Wrap this round you for a cloak," she said. "It will keep out the frost when you leave me."

The pixie was delighted. She wrapped the bit of blue silk all round her and pulled it close. "I shall get my needle and thread and make this lovely piece of silk into a proper coat with sleeves and buttons and collar," she said. "You are a dear little girl! I love you. Yes, really I do. Is there anything you would like me to give *you*?"

Millicent Mary thought hard. Then she shook her head. "No," she said at last. "There isn't anything at all, really. I've got all the toys I want. I did badly want a dolls' house, but I had one for Christmas. I don't want any sweets because I've got a tin of barley-sugar. I don't want chocolate biscuits because Mummy bought some yesterday. No – I can't think of anything."

The pixie looked most disappointed. "I do wish you'd try to think of something," she said. "Try hard!"

Millicent Mary thought again. Then she smiled. "Well," she said, "there *is* something I'd simply love – but it needs magic to do it, I think. I'd *love* it if my snowdrops could ring on my birthday, which is on February 13th!"

"Oh, that's easily managed!" said the pixie. "I'll work a spell for it. Let me see – what's your name?"

"Millicent Mary," said the little girl.

"Millicent Mary," said the pixie, writing it down in a tiny notebook. "Birthday, 13th February. Wants snowdrops to ring on that day. All right – I'll see to it! And now goodbye, my dear. I'm deliciously warm with this blue silk. See you again some day. Don't forget to listen to your snowdrops on February 13th!"

She skipped up into the air, spread her silvery wings, and flew straight out of the top of the window. Millicent Mary couldn't help feeling tremendously excited. Her birthday would soon be here – and just imagine the snowdrops ringing!

Won't she love to shake each tiny white bell, and hear it ring ting-a-ling-a-ling, ting-a-ling-a-ling! Is *your* name Millicent Mary, by any chance, and is *your* birthday on 13th February? If it is, the snowdrops will ring for you too, without a doubt – so don't forget to shake each little white bell on that day, and hear the tinkling sound they make. What a lovely surprise for all the Millicent Marys!

The engine that ran away

O nce there was a lovely wooden engine in the playroom. It was red with a blue funnel and blue wheels, and it had a dear little cab just big enough for a doll to stand inside.

At night the toys always ran to the wooden engine to ask him to give them rides round the playroom. Sometimes a doll would stand inside the cab and drive, sometimes the teddy bear and sometimes the pink rabbit.

But the wooden engine wasn't very friendly. "I don't want to give rides," he grumbled. "Get out of my cab, Teddy. I shall upset you if you try to drive me tonight. I'll run over the edge of the rug and jerk you out."

"Engines are made so that they can run along and pull things and give rides to people," said the teddy bear. "Don't be so bad tempered! It's good for you to run about at night. You'll get fat if you don't!"

"I shan't," said the engine and jerked the teddy bear so hard that he fell out. Then the toys were cross and they *all*

clambered on to the engine and made him carry every one of them.

"I shall run away," said the engine, sulkily. "I *won't* give you rides!" And will you believe it, the very next night he ran out of the playroom, down the passage, out of the garden door and into the garden!

"I'm free, I'm free!" he cried, bumping down the path. "I won't give rides any more. I'll go on a long, long journey by myself and have a lovely time!"

Now, the engine had six wooden wheels, but they were not meant to go over rough stones and tufts of grass. He went over such a big stone that quite suddenly the two back wheels came right off! The engine didn't notice it at first, and then he found that he was going rather clumsily. Oh dear – now he only had four wheels!

He went on down the path and squeezed through a hole in the fence at the bottom of the garden – but that was a silly thing to do because he broke off his funnel! He had to leave it behind, because he couldn't possibly put it on again!

On he went and on. "I feel funny without my funnel," he said to himself. "What shall I do if I ever want to send out smoke? I haven't got a funnel to blow through now!"

He bumped over a field, and suddenly ran into a big rabbit. "Hey there – what do you think *you're* doing?" cried the rabbit, angrily. "You bumped my tail."

"Get out of my way then," said the engine, rudely. That made the rabbit so angry that he chased the engine at top speed. It ran over a brick and oh dear – two more wheels broke off!

"Now I can hardly run at all," said the engine in alarm. "Oh dear, oh dear – four wheels gone, and my funnel, too. What bad luck!"

"To-whit-too-whoo!" said a big owl, flying overhead. "What's this crawling along? A new kind of rat? I'll attack it!"

And down swooped the owl and caught hold of the engine's little cab with its strong feet. The cab broke away in the owl's claws, and the poor engine hurried off without it, scared and trembling. The owl dropped the cab in disgust. "It wasn't a rat after all," it said.

The engine went on and on, and came to a very stony path indeed. Crack! Crack! Both its last wheels broke away, and the engine found itself sliding down a muddy bank, unable to stop itself. Splash! It went into a pond and floated there, looking very strange.

No wheels! No cab! Not even a funnel! Just a flat piece of wood and a round body – nothing else. No wonder the pixie who lived by the bank wondered what was falling down near her home.

"Save me, save me!" called the engine, floating away.

"Good gracious! What can it be?" said the pixie. She got a piece of string and made a loop at one end. She threw the loop over the body part of the engine and drew him back to shore. "Whatever are you?" she said.

"I'm an engine," said the poor, broken toy. "But I've lost my wheels and my cab and my funnel, so I feel very miserable indeed. I've run away, you see."

"Why did you run away?" said the pixie, drying the engine.

"Because I didn't like giving the toys a ride each night," said the engine.

"How mean of you!" said the pixie. "But I suppose you feel happier now that you have lost your six nice wheels and your cab and your lovely funnel. You can't give *anyone* a ride now."

"I *don't* feel happy," said the engine. "It's dreadful to have no wheels. And I hate not having a cab and a funnel. I wish I was back in the playroom, with all the things I've lost. I'd let the toys ride me all night long!"

"Would you really?" said the pixie. "Because if you *really* mean that I'll help you."

"I do mean it," said the engine. "I do, I do!"

Well, the pixie tied the bit of string to the body of the poor old engine and dragged it back the way he had come. First she found two wheels. Then she came to where the owl had dropped the cab. She picked that up, too. Then she found two more wheels, and soon she came to where the little blue funnel lay beside the fence. Up the garden she found the last two wheels.

"There!" she said, "I've found everything you lost. I've some magic with me and I'll put you right if you keep your promise."

"I will, truly I will," said the engine.

And then you should have seen the pixie using her magic! It was rather like blue Vaseline, and she rubbed it on the wheels and the funnel and the cab and stuck them back in their proper places.

Soon the engine felt quite himself again!

"Oh, thank you," he said, gratefully. "I feel like an engine again now. It's lovely. Can I give you a ride?"

"Oh yes!" said the pixie, and she stepped into the little cab. She could drive beautifully! She drove the engine in at the garden door, up the passage and back to the playroom. Well, well – how clever of her!

"Toys! I've brought the runaway engine back to you!" she said. "He's nice and kind now – but if he ever says he won't give you rides, look out! Because then the magic that keeps his wheels and his cab and his funnel on will vanish away – and they will all fall off on to the floor!"

And now the toys take it in turns to drive the wooden engine round and round the playroom every night – and so far he has still got all his wheels and his cab and his funnel. I do hope he doesn't lose them, don't you?

Sammy and the spider

There was once a boy called Sammy who was afraid of spiders. If he saw one running across the room he would squeal in fright.

"Don't be silly, Sammy," said his mother. "A spider can't hurt you!"

"I don't like all its legs," said Sammy.

"But my dear child, a caterpillar has plenty of legs, and you pick those up!" said his mother.

"I know," said Sammy. "But I just don't like spiders. I'm going to stamp on that one and kill it."

"Sammy, don't do that," said his mother. "Why should you take away a spider's life just because you don't happen to like it? I'd be very sorry if somebody was to stamp on *you* just because they didn't like you."

"Well – it does seem unkind," said Sammy. "But let me shoo it out of the room, Mummy!"

His mother got a shovel, let the spider run on to it, and then she dropped it out of the window.

"You must be kind to things even if you don't like them," she said. "Don't turn yourself into somebody cruel and unthinking, when you see something you are afraid of. Don't be afraid of it, and you won't feel unkind!"

"That's difficult," said Sammy. But because he knew that his mother was wise and kind herself, he tried to remember what she said.

Now one day a most enormous spider came into Sammy's bedroom. It really was a *giant*. It had eight legs, of course, and it ran like clockwork on them. Sammy stared at the spider, feeling really afraid.

"I must kill it!" he said to himself.

Then he thought again. "But after all, it can't *help* being a spider. Perhaps it would rather not be. But it has to be because it came out of a spider's egg. I shan't kill it. Mummy's right – it's bad to hurt something just because you don't happen to like it. But what shall I do with it?"

Sammy could not bear to touch the big spider. So he got his cricket bat and let the spider run on to it. Then he took the bat to the window and shook it smartly. The spider dropped off it on to the hedge below. Sammy couldn't see where it went.

"Well, that's good," he thought. "I hope it won't come back again. I'm glad I didn't stamp on it."

No more spiders came into Sammy's room that autumn, and he didn't think any more about them. Then his birthday came, and he was tremendously excited.

He had a new bicycle, with a bell, a basket, and a saddle-bag. That was simply marvellous. He had a football, and he had a toy aeroplane that really flew well.

His uncle sent him a postal order. "Buy yourself a new paintbox," he wrote in a letter. "I know you want one."

"That's just what I *do* want!" said Sammy joyfully. "Mummy, what do I do with this paper money?"

"You take it down to the post office, and they will give you money for it," said Mummy. "Take it tomorrow, because it's Saturday and you will have lots of time."

So Sammy left the paper money in his bedroom till the next day, and a dreadful thing happened! The wind came in at the window, took hold of the paper money and whisked it right away!

Sammy ran to catch it – but the wind took it out of the window at the top, where it was open. Sammy gave a yell. There was his paper money flying away on the wind!

He tore downstairs to find it. He rushed into the garden and looked on the ground everywhere. But the paper money had quite disappeared. It was a great shock for poor Sammy.

"Darling, it's no good looking any more," said Mummy, at last. "It will have blown miles away by now. There is such a tremendous wind today. Never mind. You have lots of lovely presents, and maybe someone will give you a paintbox for Christmas."

All the same Sammy was very, very sad. It was dreadful to lose the money. He had felt so rich – and now he felt so poor.

He went out into the garden to play with his football. He kicked it high into the air, and it landed on top of the privet hedge. Sammy went to get it.

And he saw a most strange and amazing sight. There was a very large web on the hedge, made by a giant of a spider, who was lurking at one end. No flies had been caught in the web – but

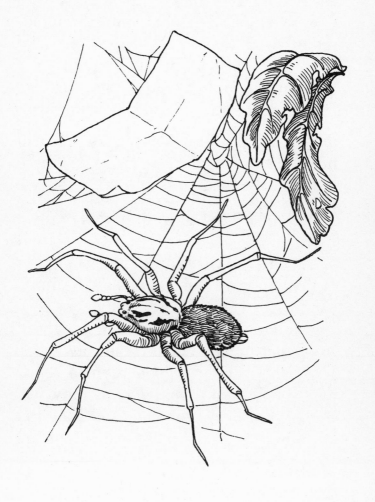

something else had been caught! Yes
– you've guessed right! Sammy's paper
money had blown right into the sticky
web, and there it was, safely held.

Sammy couldn't believe his eyes. He
stared and stared. Then he gave such
a shout that the spider ran deep into
the hedge. Sammy carefully pulled the
paper money from the web, and looked
to see if he could find the spider.

It came up to the web. It was really a
giant.

"You're the very same spider I put out
of my window weeks ago!" said Sammy.
"You are, really. And you've made a
marvellous web – and that web caught
my paper money when it blew away. So
if you like doing a good turn to repay
one done to you, spider, you may feel
happy! I'm very, very pleased I let you
go, and very, very pleased I've got my
money back!"

The spider looked at Sammy. Then it
ran into the middle of its web.

"I'm not afraid of you any more," said

Sammy. "Not one single bit. You're a friend, not an enemy! You've saved my money. I shall always like spiders after this!"

He ran indoors to tell his mother. She was simply delighted. "Well, one good turn deserves another," she said, "but I'm sure it isn't often that a spider can do a thing like *that*, Sammy!"

Sammy got his paintbox, and now he is going in for every painting competition. I wonder if he will win a prize, don't you?

The robber who wasn't there

It was a lovely spring day, and the sun shone down warmly. The primroses began to open in the garden, and George and Nora went to pick a bunch for the playroom table.

Happy, their dog, went with them. He ran round the garden, smelling here and there, just as happy as his name. He ran to the garden shed and sniffed around.

Suddenly he cocked up his ears and then began to bark madly! How he barked!

"Woof, woof, woof! Woof, woof, woof!"

"Whatever's the matter, Happy?" cried Nora, in surprise. "You'll bark your head off, then what will you do?"

"Woof, woof, woof!" barked Happy, and he scraped at the shed door with his paw.

"He wants to go in," said George. "I wonder why?"

Happy stopped barking and stood listening to something inside the shed, his head well on one side. The children listened too.

There was a noise inside the shed! It was a funny noise – a kind of scrapy, scrambly noise – and then a pot fell over and broke!

The children jumped and looked scared.

"Woof, woof, woof!" barked Happy again, and he scraped at the wooden door as if he would like to break it down.

"There's somebody hiding in there," said Nora.

"Who could it be?" said George, in a frightened whisper.

"A robber!" whispered back Nora. "Oh dear, George, I feel frightened. Let's go and tell Mummy."

They waited for a moment, and then they heard the noise inside the shed again. Another pot fell over, and the children jumped and ran away. Happy stayed behind, barking, and pawing at the door.

"There's one thing – the robber won't escape from the shed whilst Happy is barking outside," panted George, as the two children ran to the house.

"No – so he's a prisoner till we get somebody to catch him!" said Nora.

They rushed into the house and called for their mother. "Mummy! Mummy! Come quickly! Where are you?"

But Mummy was out. So they ran to tell Jane their big sister. "Jane! Jane! There's a robber in the garden shed!" said George. "Will you come and catch him?"

"Good gracious, no!" cried Jane, quite alarmed. "I'm certainly not going robber-catching! I'll tell Cook!"

So Jane, George and Nora ran to the kitchen to tell the cook about the robber in the garden shed. Cook was surprised to see them all running at top speed into her kitchen.

"What's the matter?" she said.

"Oh, Cook, there's a robber in the garden shed!" panted Jane. "Get your rolling pin and come and catch him."

"Indeed, I won't," said Cook at once. "A robber should be caught by the policeman. He'll be by here soon. We'll watch for him and tell him. Fancy that now – a robber in the garden shed!"

"Happy is keeping him prisoner till we get somebody to catch the robber," said Nora, feeling tremendously excited. "Can't you hear him barking like mad?"

They could. "Woof, woof, woof!"

"Here comes the policeman!" said Cook at last, and they saw the big burly policeman walking slowly down their road. George, Nora, Jane, and Cook all flew out to the front gate and called to him.

"Oh, Mr Policeman! We've got a robber here!"

"What did you say?" asked the policeman in great surprise, and he took out his notebook and pencil.

"Oh, there's no time to be writing notes," cried Jane. "There's a robber in the garden shed and the dog's guarding him. He'll be a very fierce robber, and maybe he'll fight you, Mr Policeman. Hadn't you better get someone to help you?"

"Oh no," said the policeman, rather grandly. "I'm quite used to robbers."

So George, Nora, Jane, Cook, and the policeman all went down the garden to the shed, where Happy was still barking.

"Now just listen, everyone!" said George.

So they all listened, and sure enough they could hear the noise in the shed all right – and two more pots fell over with a crash! Even the policeman jumped, and as for Jane, she ran half-way up the garden in fright.

"Now here's a strange thing," said

the policeman, suddenly pointing to the door. "It's locked on the outside, there's the key in the lock, and it's turned! Now how did the robber get in there, and yet lock the door on the outside?"

Everybody stared at the lock, but nobody could think how a robber could lock himself in and yet leave the key outside. It was a mystery.

The policeman unlocked the door and shouted out in a loud, stern voice, "Come out, there! Come out at once!"

Everyone waited to see who would come out – but nobody did! Another plant pot fell over. The policeman grew angry.

"Am I to come in after you? Come out at once!" But still nobody came out. So the policeman bravely stuck his head inside the dark shed and looked around.

"There's nobody here!" he said in the greatest astonishment. "Well – that's odd!"

Everybody looked inside – and sure

enough there was no robber there at all. Happy darted round and round the shed, sniffing happily. Everyone went out again and talked hard.

"Then who made that noise?"

"There *was* somebody there!"

"And it must have been a robber!"

"How could he have got away?"

And suddenly they heard the noise again! They all stared at the door, feeling quite scared.

Then the robber walked out! Yes – he really did! And who do you suppose it was? Why, nobody else but Crawler, the old tortoise, who had been put there asleep in a box for the winter! He had woken up, scrambled out of his box, and crawled round the shed, knocking over pots as he went. Well, well, well!

He walked out into the warm spring sunshine, and blinked his eyes at everyone. Happy danced round him, barking. Everyone went red and looked foolish.

Then George laughed – and Nora

joined in. Jane giggled and Cook roared. The policeman opened his mouth and ha-ha-ha'd too. It was surprising to hear them, and Crawler the tortoise was frightened. He popped his head under his shell!

"The robber who wasn't there!" cried Nora, pointing to the tortoise. "Oh, Crawler, what a fright you gave us!"

A pair of pickles

Billy and Bessie were a pair of pickles. You never knew what mischief they would be up to next!

They dirtied their clothes every day. They lost things. They came in muddy and never thought of wiping their shoes. Well, really, I can't tell you half the things they did, because I would need about ten books to put them in!

Everybody called them "the Pickles". "Where are those Pickles?" Mummy would say at dinner time. "It is time they were home."

"Hello, Pickles!" people would say. Billy and Bessie thought it was fun to be two pickles. They didn't think of the worry they made for their mother.

Now one day a funny little fellow came wandering into our land. He was helper to Mister Grumpy-Wumps, the enchanter of Heyho Wood, and Mister Grumpy-Wumps was in one of his tempers.

He always was on Mondays, because he had cold meat for dinner, and he hated it.

"Cold meat again!" he would shout to his helper. "How dare you!"

"Well, it's Monday," said the helper. "And everyone has cold meat on Monday, sir."

"Well, give me something nice to eat with it!" shouted the enchanter. So sometimes the helper gave him beetroot, sometimes he gave him tomato sauce or celery, and sometimes horseradish and cream.

And then one day Mister Grumpy-Wumps took it into his head to want pickles!

"Pickles!" said the helper in surprise. "I've never heard of them. Can't have pickles, Mister Grumpy-Wumps!"

"How dare you tell me that I can't have something I want!" roared Grumpy-Wumps, and for a moment he looked so fierce that he quite startled the little helper. "Go out and bring me pickles. Don't dare to come back till you've got them!"

"Where do I get them?" asked the helper, putting on his hat.

"How do I know?" said the enchanter. "They may grow on trees. They may be sold in a shop. They may sit on chimney-pots. They may walk about in the fields. Anyway, go and get some."

So that was how the little helper happened to come wandering into our land, looking for pickles. And it so happened that he met Bessie and Billy, who were in mischief as usual, paddling in the muddy pond.

"Hello!" said the little fellow.

"Hello!" said the Pickles.

"I'm looking for something," said the

helper. "Can you help me, I wonder? I'm looking for pickles."

Billy laughed. "*We* are pickles!" he said.

"Don't be silly," said the little man sharply.

"I'm not silly," said Billy. "Anybody will tell you we're pickles. Go and ask that lady over there."

The lady was the wife of the farmer. The little man went over to her and raised his hat politely. "Could you please tell me if those two children are pickles?" he asked.

"They certainly are!" said the farmer's wife, with a smile. "Real pickles!"

"Thank you," said the helper, puzzled. So the children *were* pickles. Well, well, well! He would have to take them to Mister Grumpy-Wumps, that's all.

So he went back to them and took them firmly by the hands. "You must come with me," he said. "My master, Mister Grumpy-Wumps, always has cold meat for his dinner on Mondays, and today is Monday, and he told me to go and get him pickles to eat with his dinner. So I'm afraid you must come."

"We won't! We won't!" cried Bessie. "We're not the kind of pickles you eat! Let us go!"

But the helper wouldn't. No, he made the two Pickles go with him to his own land, and he took them right to the enchanter's castle and led them up to Mister Grumpy-Wumps.

"I've brought you the Pickles," he said.

The enchanter stared at the children in dismay. He was really a very kind-hearted fellow, and he knew he couldn't possibly eat this sort of pickle. Well, well! To think that children were pickles! What a very astonishing thing!

"Please don't think we're pickles to eat," said Billy. "We're not!"

"That lady you pointed out to me said you *were*!" said the helper. "She said you were real pickles."

"Well," said the enchanter, going

rather red, "somehow I don't feel like pickles today. Take the children back, you silly man and when I feel like pickles again, you can fetch them. But today I really don't. I think I'll have beetroot instead."

"How you do change your mind!" grumbled the helper, going to fetch the beetroot. As soon as he was out of the room the children ran through another door and tore home as fast as ever they could. They didn't know how glad Mister Grumpy-Wumps was to see them go! Good gracious! How could anyone eat pickles like that!

When they got home the children sat down quietly in a corner. "I'm going to stop being naughty enough to be called a pickle," whispered Bessie to Billy. "After all, we do upset Mummy when we get so dirty and our clothes so torn. Let's be good for a change."

So now they are really very good, and Mummy can't imagine why. She also doesn't know where one of her jars of home-made pickles has gone to, that the children begged from her. But *I* know! It's hidden inside a hollow tree ready to give to the little helper if ever he comes hunting for pickles again.

"He shan't make a mistake *next* time!" says Billy. What a treat for old Grumpy-Wumps when he tastes *real* pickles!

Mollie's mud-pies

It was very hot, so hot that Mollie wore only a swimsuit. It was nearly summer, and Mummy said if it was so hot now, whatever would it be like in the middle of summer.

"It's nice," said Mollie, who liked wearing almost nothing. She didn't even wear shoes in the garden. "I like it, Mummy. I do wish we were by the sea, then I could swim."

"Well, I'll tell you what I will do," said her mother. "I will water you each night before you go to bed!"

"Water me!" said Mollie, in surprise. "What do you mean, Mummy?"

"Just what I say," said Mummy. "I'll fill a can with half-warm water, and

then water you before you go to bed.
That will be fun for you."

"Oh, *yes*," said Mollie in delight. "I
should love that."

She played in the hot garden. The
grass looked yellow, not green.
Everywhere was dried up and dusty.
Mollie wondered if the birds had any
puddles to drink from. They must be
thirsty now, with all the puddles dried
up. So she filled a little bowl with water,
and set it out on the grass. It was fun to
see the birds coming to drink from it.

"They drink so sweetly," said Mollie.
"They dip in their beaks, and then hold
their heads back, Mummy, and let the
water run down their throats."

When the evening came, Mummy
filled a big watering-can with half-
warm water, and called Mollie. "Come
and have your watering!"

"Will it make me grow, like the
flowers?" cried Mollie, dancing about.
Mummy tipped up the can. Mollie gave
a squeal. Although the water was not

cold, it felt cold on her hot little body. She danced about, squeaking with excitement and joy.

"The water's made a nice muddy patch on the path," she cried. "Look, my toes are brown and muddy with dancing in it."

"You'll have to wash them well," said Mummy, filling the can again. "Come along – one more watering and you must go to bed."

The patch of path was indeed wet and muddy after the second can of water had been poured all over Mollie. "If it's wet tomorrow, I shall make little mud-pies of it," said Mollie.

It was still muddy the next day. After breakfast Mollie went to the mud and dabbled her fingers in it. "I shall make little pies and cakes of mud, and set them in the sun to dry," she thought. "That will be a nice game to play."

Mummy called her. "If you want to play that dirty game you must wear an overall over that nice clean swimsuit. Come along."

Mollie ran indoors. When she came out again she found someone else in her mud-patch! It was a little bird with a touch of white at the foot of his dark, long tail, and underneath his body. He stared at Mollie, and then scraped up some mud in his beak.

"Oh!" said Mollie, pleased. "Are you making mud-pies too? I never knew a bird liked playing with mud before. Do play with me."

The little bird gave a twitter, filled his beak quite full, and then suddenly darted into the air on curving wings.

Mollie saw that he had a forked tail behind him.

"I wish he hadn't gone," she thought. "It would have been fun to play with him. I suppose he has taken the mud to make mud-pies somewhere else."

Suddenly the little bird came back again. He looked at Mollie, and she looked at him. He wondered if Mollie was the kind of child to throw stones at him, or to shout and frighten him away.

But she wasn't. She was like you. She liked birds, and wanted them to stay close to her so that she could watch them and make friends with them.

She sat quite still and watched him. He went to the mud again, and began to scrape up some more. Then another bird, exactly like him, flew down, and he began to dabble in it as well. Mollie was delighted.

"Everyone is making mud-pies this morning," she said. "Gracious – here's another! How busy they all are in my muddy patch. I'll get busy too."

Once the birds had made up their minds that Mollie was a friend, they became very busy indeed. They filled their little beaks with mud time after time, and then flew away round the house. Mollie wondered where they went. They kept coming and going all the morning.

"Funny little mud-pie birds," she said to them. "Do you bake your mud-pies up on the roof somewhere? I bake mine here, look!"

The hot sun baked her pies beautifully. She put them on a plate out of her tea-set and took them in to her mummy.

"Have a mud-pie?" she said. "They are lovely. And, oh, Mummy, the mud-pie birds have played in the mud with me all morning. They were sweet."

Mummy was surprised. "Mud-pie birds! Whatever do you mean?"

"Well, they came and played with my mud and took some away to make mud-pies with. I expect they baked them up on the roof," said Mollie.

Mummy thought it was a little tale of Mollie's. She pretended to eat Mollie's mud-pie, and then offered Mollie a bun from the oven.

"I've been baking too," she said. "Have a hot bun? And now I think you had better stop playing with the mud and wash yourself."

"The mud is gone now," said Mollie. "The sun has baked it hard."

The little birds didn't come into the garden any more that day. "I suppose they only came for the mud," thought Mollie. "Well, if Mummy waters me again tonight there will be more mud tomorrow for us all to play with."

There was – a nice big patch – and down came the little birds again, to scrape up the mud. Mollie was so pleased.

"It's nice to have you to play with me," she said to the busy little birds. "But I really wish you would tell me what you do with your mud."

They twittered a little song to her, high and sweet, but she didn't understand what they said. They flew to and from the mud all morning, till the sun dried it up.

"Mummy, why do the mud-pie birds take my mud?" asked Mollie. "I do want to know. I didn't know that birds like mud so much."

Her daddy was there, and he looked up from his newspaper. "What's all this about mud-pie birds?" he asked. So Mollie told him.

"Ah," he said. "Now I know what birds you mean. Your mud-pie birds are house-martins, cousins of the pretty swallows we see flying high in the air all summer."

"House-martins!" said Mollie. "*I* should call them mud-martins. What do they do with my mud?"

"Come with me and I'll show you," said Daddy. He took Mollie's hand, and led her upstairs. They went into her

bedroom. Daddy went to the window and opened it wide.

"Now look out of your window, above it, to the edge of the roof overhead," he said. "Tell me what you see."

Mollie leaned out, and looked up. She gave a cry. "Oh, Daddy! The mud-pie birds are there. They are making something of my mud. What is it?"

"It's a nest," said Daddy. "The house-martins don't use dead leaves and twigs and moss for their nests as most birds do. They make them of mud. They fetch beakfuls of mud, and plaster it against the wall, gradually building it out till they have made a fine nest of mud, with a hole to get in and out. There's the hole in that nest. Look!"

As Mollie watched, one of the little birds flew up with his beak full of mud from somewhere, and pressed it against the edge of his nest.

"There you are," said Daddy. "He brings wet mud, and it dries hard in the sun, making a perfectly good nest for his little wife to lay her eggs in, and have her young ones."

"Oh, Daddy! Fancy making a nest of my mud, the mud that was made when Mummy watered me each evening," said Mollie in delight. "I couldn't think why the mud-birds came to make mud-pies. I did not know they were making mud-nests – and over my bedroom window, too, tucked under the edge of the roof! I shall hear them calling and twittering to each other all day long. Look – there's another nest farther along. You won't pull them down, will you?"

"Of course not!" said Daddy, who was fond of birds. "They can nest there in peace and happiness, out of reach of the cats. Later on we shall see their young ones popping their heads out of the holes in the mud-nests."

And so they did! The house-martins laid eggs in their strange mud-nests, and in a few weeks' time Mollie saw three or four tiny feathery heads popping out of the hole in the nest above her window, waiting for the father and mother to come back with flies to feed them.

Later still the little birds flew into the sky with their mother and father, learning how to dart and soar and glide, and how to catch the hundreds of insects that flew in the air. Daddy said they did a great deal of good, because the flies were a pest.

And then one day they were all gone. Mollie looked into the sky and they were not there.

"They've gone away south, where it

is warmer," said Daddy. "There will be plenty of insects for them to eat there. Our winter is coming and they do not like that."

"I don't want them to go away," said Mollie sadly.

"Well, they will be back again in the spring," said Daddy. "And, Mollie, if the weather is hot and dry again when they come back, you must make a muddy patch once more, and they will come to it, and build their nest again over your window. They love to come back to exactly the same place, if they can."

So, of course, Mollie is going to watch for them when the spring comes. You must watch too, and if we have hot and dry weather in May, when the mud-pie birds want to build their nests, you can do as Mollie did – make a muddy patch for them, and watch them fly down to it to fill their beaks.

Maybe they will build a mud-nest over your window, too. That really would be fun, wouldn't it?

Tiptap's little trick

M r Twisty went to market every Friday with two big baskets of goods to sell. In one basket he took vegetables or fruit, and in the other he took eggs.

"Old Twisty helps himself to other people's fruit and vegetables and eggs at night," said the people of the village. "He comes in the dark, like a shadow – and pulls up our lettuces and picks our peas and our fruit. He goes into our hen-houses and takes the eggs, as sly as a rat in the night!"

But nobody could catch old Twisty at it, nobody at all. He was as full of tricks and wily ways as a weasel.

"We'll have to play a trick on *him*,"

said Dame Ho-Ho at last. "So let's think hard."

They thought and they thought. Mr Flap frowned and Mr Flop scowled, they thought so hard. Mother Run-Round and old Mrs Scatter did their best to think of a way to trick Twisty and pay him back for his mean ways.

It was little Tiptap who thought of an idea. He told the others, and they laughed. "It's a bit silly," said Dame Ho-Ho, "but it *might* catch him."

"It's good," said Mr Flap. "We'll try it."

So the next day, when everyone was going to market, little Tiptap went, too. He had some strong rope coiled round his waist, and he laughed as he went.

He ran round a corner, tied the end of the rope to something there, and then came back again, holding his end. He waited till he saw Mr Twisty coming along with two heavy baskets.

Then Tiptap began to tug and pull at the rope for all he was worth. "Come up, there!" he yelled. "Come along, will you! Why won't you come? You'll be late for market and I won't be able to sell you. Come on, there!"

Mr Twisty stopped, put down his baskets and watched. He liked seeing people in difficulties.

Tiptap tugged and tugged at the rope which was stretched as tight as could be. "Come along, I tell you!" he cried. "Acting like this on market day!"

"Ha-ha!" laughed Mr Twisty. "Ho-ho! Your pig – or your cow or whatever it is – wants to go a different way from you. Ho-ho! He'll pull *you* round the corner soon!"

Everyone was watching Tiptap. Dame Ho-Ho was there, smiling. Mr Flap and Mr Flop stood there, nodding in delight. Mother Run-Round and Mrs Scatter laughed loudly.

"All of you laughing at me and not giving a hand to help!" cried Tiptap, pulling hard. "Help, somebody!"

Mother Run-Round came up to help.

She tugged and pulled, too, but it wasn't any good. No animal came round the corner on the end of the rope.

"*Will* you come along?" shouted Tiptap, in a very angry voice. "I tell you, if you don't come I'll sell you for five pounds, here and now! I'm tired of you!"

Twisty pricked up his ears. What! Tiptap was so angry that he would sell this animal cheaply? Well, perhaps Twisty could get a good bargain.

"Here – I'll pull it round for you," he said. "And, if you like, I'll buy the creature. It will save you going to the market. But a stubborn, bad-tempered animal like this won't be worth much."

"You're right," said Tiptap, tugging. "If it's going to act like this at every corner I'll never get to market. You can have it for five pounds."

"Say three," said Twisty, and he took the rope-end from Tiptap. He pulled. My word – what animal could there be at the end of this rope? He couldn't budge

it! It must at least be a cow – or even a horse or donkey! He tugged and tugged. Yes – it must be a horse.

"Say four pounds," said Tiptap, "and your two baskets of goods. You won't want to carry those to market if you've got something else to tug along."

"A horse for four pounds!" thought Twisty in delight, still pulling hard. He turned to Tiptap.

"All right. Feel in my pocket and take four pounds. You can have the baskets, too."

"Thanks!" said Tiptap, and winked at everyone in delight. He picked up the baskets and looked into them. "Ah – these eggs must be yours, Mr Flap and Mr Flop. And these lettuces must belong to you, Mother Run-Round. They are just like you grow. And these . . ."

"You stop talking like that!" yelled Mr Twisty, in a rage. But he couldn't run after Tiptap because he didn't dare to leave go of the rope!

Tiptap and the others went off giggling. Mr Twisty nearly went mad trying to pull the rope hard enough to pull the animal to him.

Suddenly someone appeared at the corner. It was Mr Letters, the postman. He shouted at Mr Twisty.

"Hey, you! What do you think you're doing? You've nearly pulled the letter-box down. Is this a joke, or what?"

Mr Twisty stared at him. He ran quickly to the corner and looked round it. My, oh my – that rope was tied firmly round a stout red letter-box – and it was almost bent in half with Twisty's pulling! He gaped at it.

"B-b-b-but there should be a horse, or a cow or a pig, on the end of the rope," stammered Mr Twisty in dismay.

"Well, it must have turned into a letter-box, then," said Mr Letters. "And I'm afraid I must ask you to come to the police-station with me, Mr Twisty, on a charge of doing malicious damage to a public letter-box! That's for posting letters in, not for pulling down!"

Mr Twisty didn't wait a moment. He fled at top speed, caught the first bus he saw, and went to the Village of Far-Away. What with animals that turned into letter-boxes – and postmen that wanted to take him away – and everyone laughing at him – he just couldn't stay another moment.

The folk of the village saw him going by at top speed to catch the bus. How they laughed!

Tiptap divided the four pounds between everyone who had goods stolen from them by Twisty. And what do you think they did with it? They put it together again and gave a party for Tiptap!

"You got rid of mean old Twisty," they said. "You deserve a party, Tiptap. He'll never dare to come back again."

They were right. He never did.

Old Mister Glue-Pot

Old Mister Glue-Pot was a gnome who lived in Pillywee Village, on the borders of Fairyland. He kept a paint shop and sold paint in pots, and also very sticky brown glue.

He made this glue himself, and it was so strong that just a touch of it would stick two broken pieces of a jar or dish together in a trice. Mister Glue-Pot had made a lot of money out of this very strong glue.

In fact, he had made such a lot of money that he really didn't bother very much about his shop. He put Snubby the pixie in charge of it, and then he went into his parlour, put his feet up on the mantelpiece, and slept peacefully.

Snubby was not a good shopkeeper. He played about too much. He painted the walls of the shop green and yellow, with blue spots – and will you believe it, Mister Glue-Pot never noticed! Then Snubby discovered the glue. What a game he had with it!

First of all he got some on his hands by mistake – and, dear me, whatever

Snubby touched stuck fast to him. He touched a newspaper and that stuck. He touched two pencils and those stuck! He touched Mister Glue-Pot's best Sunday hat and that stuck. Soon you could hardly see Snubby because so many things were sticking to him!

Snubby managed to unstick himself at last. He stood looking at Mister Glue-Pot's big barrel of glue and grinned. He would have a few jokes with that!

He peeled an orange and then carefully dabbed a spot of glue on each bit of peel. When no one was looking the naughty pixie slipped out of the shop and pressed each bit of peel on the pavement. They all stuck fast. Snubby knew that Mister Plod-Plod, the policeman, would come along that way in a few minutes' time – and old Plod-Plod would certainly try to pick up all those bits of peel!

"It will be fun to see him pulling at them," giggled the naughty pixie to himself. He pressed his snubby nose against the shop window and waited. Soon he heard the plod-plod-plod noise that the policeman's feet made. Up came Mister Plod-Plod and saw the orange peel.

"Now, who's been dropping orange peel about?" he said in his crossest voice. "It is forbidden to do such a thing!"

He looked all round but he could see no one. So Mister Plod-Plod stooped down to pick up all the bits himself – but they were stuck fast to the pavement! Plod-Plod pulled and tugged, and then stared at the peel in amazement. Was it magic? Why wouldn't it come off the pavement?

Plod-Plod took out his knife and cut all the peel away. He put it in his pocket and walked off, looking very puzzled and angry. Snubby laughed till his sides ached.

"That was a good trick!" he said. "Now what else shall I do?"

But before he could do anything else Mister Plod-Plod came back again and asked to see Mister Glue-Pot.

"Mister Glue-Pot," he said sternly, "did you know that someone has been using your glue to stick bits of orange peel to the pavement?"

"Dear me, no!" said Glue-Pot.

"Well, they have," said Plod-Plod. "Please see that you keep an eye on your glue-barrel, Glue-Pot."

"Certainly, certainly," said the old fellow, and he called Snubby to him. "Look after the glue-barrel very, very carefully," he said. Snubby grinned and nodded. He would look after it all right!

Now next door to Mister Glue-Pot's shop was a baker's shop, and outside the door was a very fine mat for people to wipe their feet on. Snubby thought it would be a great joke to dab some glue on it – and then everyone's feet would get stuck there. What fun that would be!

So that night he slipped out with a brush full of glue and daubed the whole mat with it. And you should have seen the muddle there was at the baker's next day!

Dame Trit-Trot and Mister Top-hat went to the baker's shop at the same time, and both trod on the mat together. That was all right – but when they tried to walk off it into the shop they couldn't. The mat went with them! Poor Dame Trit-Trot slipped and slid, trying to get her feet off the sticky mat, and Mister Top-hat suddenly lost his balance and sat down. That was worse than ever! It took the baker two hours to untangle Trit-Trot, Top-hat, and the mat.

How angry they all were! They marched into Mister Glue-Pot's shop and banged on the counter so loudly that Mister Glue-Pot, who was fast asleep in the parlour, woke up, leapt out of his chair, and trod on his poor cat. She scratched him hard and naughty Snubby laughed till he cried.

"If you don't look after your glue better, we shall punish you, Glue-Pot!" cried Trit-Trot, Top-hat, and the baker.

They told him about the sticky mat, and Glue-Pot was full of horror to think that his glue should be used for tricks like that.

"Just see you look after the glue-barrel even better than before," he said to Snubby. And Snubby grinned and said he would. But, the very next day, Snubby slipped across the road to the sweet-shop when it was empty, and dabbed the three chairs with the glue. Oh, what a dreadful thing to do!

That afternoon Snubby watched the people going in to buy sweets. He saw Mrs Lightfoot sit down on a chair. He saw Mister Tap-Tap. He saw the old brownie, Longbeard, sitting down too. They talked together for a little while till their sweets were ready – then they tried to get up to go.

But their chairs stuck to them! They ran out of the shop in horror, taking the chairs with them, though the shopkeeper shouted to them to bring them back. They ran down the street

with the chairs knocking behind them —
and they ran straight into Mister Plod-
Plod, the policeman. And it wasn't long
before he found that it was Mister Glue-
Pot's glue that had done the mischief
again.

He went straight to the paint-shop
and shouted for Mister Glue-Pot.

"Pack up your things, take your glue and leave Pillywee Village," he ordered. "We have had enough of these glue tricks, Mister Glue-Pot. Take this cheeky little pixie with you, for I shouldn't be surprised if he had done the mischief."

So poor Mister Glue-Pot and Snubby had to pack up and go. Snubby had to carry the barrel of glue on his back, for Mister Plod-Plod wouldn't let him leave it behind. So over the borders of Fairyland it was carried, and it's still somewhere about today.

Do you know what it is used for? Snubby and Glue-Pot sell it to the chestnut trees in the early spring, so that their buds can be painted with glue to prevent the frost from pinching them. Isn't that a good idea? Snubby paints each bud. You may see him if you look, but if you can't see him, pick a chestnut twig and feel how very strong Mister Glue-Pot's glue is. You *will* be surprised!

Goodbye Master Meddle

Meddle always liked roaming round the railway station. It was a most exciting place, with trains puffing in and out, people hurrying all about, and porters shouting, "Mind your backs, please!"

One morning he went into the station, and sat down on a seat to watch what was going on. He saw the people buying their tickets, carrying their luggage, looking for their trains.

"They all look very *worried*," said Meddle to himself. "Very worried indeed. Perhaps I'd better help some of them."

Now, Meddle, as you know, was exactly like his name. If he *could* poke his long nose into anything and meddle with it, he was happy! So up he got to see what he could do.

He met a little man panting and puffing, carrying a very heavy bag. Meddle went up to him and tried to get hold of it. "Let me help," he said.

"Certainly not. Let go," said the man, fiercely. "I know what you'd do if I let you take my bag – run off with it! And that's the last I would see of it."

"What a dreadful thing to say!" said Meddle, and stalked off crossly. He bumped into a woman who was carrying three parcels and dragging a little dog along too. "Allow me, Madam!" said Meddle politely, and took the biggest parcel from the woman.

The dog immediately flew at him and nipped his leg. Meddle dropped the parcel and howled. There was a crash!

"There now!" said the woman, angrily. "I had my best glass bowls packed in that parcel! What do you

think you are doing, snatching it from me?"

"Your horrible dog bit me," said Meddle, most annoyed.

"Well, of course he did!" said the woman. "He thought you were stealing my parcel. It served you right. Please call a porter and ask him to clear up this mess of broken glass – and you will have to pay me five pounds for breaking the bowls."

A porter came up. "*I* saw you meddling!" he said to Meddle. "If parcels want carrying, *I'll* carry them. It's my job, not yours. And *you* can clear up the mess, because that's your job, not mine!"

Well, you would have thought that Meddle would have had enough of poking his nose into other people's affairs by then, wouldn't you? Not a bit of it! He apologized to the angry woman, he cleared up the mess – and then he went around looking for somebody else to meddle with.

He saw a little man, a big, plump woman, and four children all trailing along. "Oh dear, oh dear!" said the woman. "We shall miss the train, I know! Where do we get our tickets?"

"Madam, over there," said Meddle, hurrying up to her. "Shall I hold the children's hands while you get them?"

"No, thank you," said the woman. "They can hold each other's hands. Dad, get your money ready for the tickets. Oh dear, what a queue there is at the ticket-office!"

"Madam, you go and get your seats in the train, and I'll buy the tickets for you," said Meddle.

"Do go away!" said the little man, crossly. "I'm not leaving you here with my money, I wouldn't be so silly!"

"That's not a nice thing to say at all!" said Meddle, most offended. "Do you mean to say I'd run off with the money? Well, I never heard such a –"

"Do please go away," said the plump woman. "We can look after ourselves all right. Oh my, oh my, what a queue. I wish these people in front of us would hurry up, I know we shall miss our train."

"We'll catch it all right," said the little man, looking at the station clock. "But if it's crowded we shan't get any seats, that's certain."

The children began to cry. "I want a seat," sobbed one. "I want to look out of the window."

"Shall I go and get some seats for you?" said Meddle, quite determined to help in some way. "I could go and find a carriage and put newspapers and things on six seats — then no one would take those seats, and when you came along you could have them. I could hop out of the carriage and wave goodbye."

"What an extraordinary fellow!" said the little man to his wife. He turned to Meddle. "I tell you, we don't want people poking their noses into our business," he said. "We can't stop you finding seats, of course, and spreading them with newspapers and coats to keep them for us! I can see you mean to interfere with us in *some* way!"

"Not interfere – just *help*," said Meddle, quite hurt. "All right – I'm off to get some seats for you. I'll buy some newspapers to spread on them, so that people will know they are all reserved for others!"

He hurried away, pleased. He bought some papers and then ran to find the train. Bother! He had forgotten to ask which one it was. It must be the very next train leaving, because the little man and his wife were in such a hurry to get the tickets. One of the children had said they were going to the sea – now which train would it be?

"Ah – here's one leaving in five minutes – to Seaside Town," said Meddle. "This must be it. How glad they will be when they come rushing on to the platform, find the train is full – but with six seats saved for them!"

He bought a platform ticket and

hurried to the train. He found a carriage that was quite empty. Good! He sat down, and arranged four newspapers and his overcoat on five seats. He sat in the sixth himself, of course.

He felt pleased with himself. "It's so nice to help people," he said. "Now that little family will all travel comfortably to the seaside, each with a nice seat all the way."

People looked into the carriage, saw the newspapers and coat on the seats and went on again. Meddle grinned. Aha! He had been very clever, he thought.

The minutes went by. Meddle began to feel anxious. Surely those people wouldn't miss the train? He looked out of the door. There was no sign of them. Oh dear – should he go and hurry them up?

Meddle got out some pennies to buy some chocolate on his way out. One fell from his hand and rolled under the seat. Oh dear! Meddle got down. It was in the far corner. Meddle had to get halfway under the seat to reach it.

A loud whistle blew. PHEEEEEEEE! Meddle jumped. He tried to wriggle out from under the seat, but somehow or other he got stuck. "Wait, wait! Tell the engine not to go yet!" shouted Meddle, from under the seat. But nobody heard him, of course. The engine began to puff out smoke and then, with a rattle and a rumble and clatter, the train began to pull out of the station!

Meddle wriggled himself free and rushed to the window. He leaned out, shouting loudly, trying to open the door. It was a good thing he couldn't, because the train was now going quite fast.

"Stop! Stop! Let me out!" yelled Meddle. "I'm not going, I tell you!"

But he was. He couldn't help it! And the last thing that poor Meddle saw was the little man and his family all getting into a train marked 'To Golden Sands' – and finding plenty of seats, too!

"This *wasn't* their train!" groaned

poor Meddle. "And *what* will the ticket-inspector say to me if he comes and finds me without a proper ticket and all the seats to myself? Oh dear – this is what comes of helping people."

No, Meddle – that's what comes of meddling! There he goes, all the way to the sea, first stop Seaside Town.

Mr Stamp-About in a fix

"I've written three times to Mr Tiles to tell him to come and mend my roof!" said Mr Stamp-About to his sister. "And what does he say? He says he's too busy! Pah! Too busy to mend *my* roof! Just wait till I see him!"

"Please don't stamp on that rug," said his sister. "You're making the dust fly about. I think it's because you're so bad-tempered that people won't come and do things for you. Now stop stamping. If you *want* to beat the dust out of that rug, take it out, hang it over the line and beat it."

"Pah!" said Mr Stamp-About, and stalked out of the room. He put on his hat and went to find Mr Tiles. He found

him in a shed, getting together his tools to go and do a job.

Mr Stamp-About caught hold of him. "Ha! I suppose you were just about to come and mend my roof! Now don't you dare to say you weren't! You come along with me this minute!"

Little Mr Tiles looked at the big, fierce Mr Stamp-About. "Let go," he said. "If you force me to go with you like this I'll have to come – but I won't put your tiles on properly, so there!"

"Oh, yes, you will!" said Mr Stamp-About. "Because I'll sit by you and watch you! And not a penny will you get if you don't do your best work. Now bring some tiles along with you, and a pot of paint, too, to touch up the gutters. And I shall sit on a chimney-pot and watch you!"

"You will, will you?" said little Mr Tiles. "Right. I'll get the tiles – here they are. And I'll bring this pot and this brush along with me. Off we go!"

And off they went together,

Mr Stamp-About holding on fast to Mr Tiles in case he ran off. But he didn't. He walked along quite amiably, and talked about the weather.

"Fetch the ladder," said Mr Stamp-About, when they got to his house. "It's in my shed. Climb up it first and begin to put on the new tiles. I'm going to have a cup of hot cocoa as it's a cold day. Then I'll come up the ladder, and sit on a chimney-pot to watch you. I'll have a fine view of your work, I can tell you!"

Mr Tiles went to fetch the ladder. He set it up against the gutter and climbed up. Mr Stamp-About had disappeared into the house to get his cocoa. Dear, dear – he hadn't even thought of offering cold Mr Tiles a cup. Still, that suited Mr Tiles all right. He had something to do before Mr Stamp-About came out again!

He climbed the ladder quickly, taking his tiles with him. He set them down on the roof and then went back for his pot and his brush. He grinned as he brought those up. He took a quick look down. Mr Stamp-About was nowhere to be seen. He was somewhere in the house, having cocoa and biscuits!

Mr Tiles looked at the two chimneys sticking up out of the roof. One was smoking. One wasn't, so that was the one that Mr Stamp-About would sit on to watch Mr Tiles doing his work! Aha!

Mr Tiles climbed up to the chimney-pot. It was squat and round. He took his brush and dipped it into his pot. He painted the rim of the pot round and round and round.

But not with paint. Oh, no! There was no paint in that pot – there was glue. Nice, sticky glue! Aha, Mr Stamp-About, you didn't know that, did you, because the pot was labelled "White Paint"!

Mr Tiles grinned. He slid down to where the roof needed new tiles and set to work. Presently he heard Mr Stamp-About climbing up the ladder. He saw him clambering up to the chimney-pot and sitting himself flat down on it, just as if it were a stool. Mr Tiles grinned to himself.

"Now, get on, Tiles," said Stamp-About. "I can see everything you do. You're to work well and quickly. I'm not going to pay you too much, either."

"You're going to pay me twenty pounds," said Mr Tiles. "Or your sister is. Twenty pounds, Mr Stamp-About – part-payment for this work, and part-payment for your bad temper!"

If Mr Stamp-About hadn't been stuck fast to the chimney-pot he would have fallen off in rage. He stamped his feet on the roof and loosened another tile.

"That's no good!" said Mr Tiles. "That will cost you even more for another tile. Still, stamp about, Stamp-About. I don't mind you paying me more money!"

Stamp-About shouted, roared and stamped. Mr Tiles took no notice. He finished his work and went down the ladder. "Twenty one pounds!" he shouted to Stamp-About. "I'll get it from your sister as I'm sure you won't give it to me!"

Mr Stamp-About tried to get up from his chimney-pot seat, but he couldn't. Something seemed to be holding him back. What *could* it be?

"Come back! Don't you dare to ask my sister to pay you!" he yelled. "I'll pay you ten pounds and that's too much!"

"Goodbye," said Mr Tiles, jumping off the ladder. "Be careful you don't loosen any more tiles!"

He went into the house and told Stamp-About's sister she was to pay him twenty one pounds. She took it out of the cash box and gave it to him. He beamed and went out.

"Where's my brother?" called the sister. "I must just be certain the amount is right."

"He won't come in for a bit," said Mr Tiles with a grin. "You can ask him then."

Off he went, looking back now and again to see the furious Mr Stamp-About. There he sat on the chimney, trying his best to get up, but the glue was much too strong for him. He raged and stamped and shouted, and soon a collection of interested people came to watch.

"I'm stuck, I'm stuck!" he yelled. "Get me down!"

But people were afraid of his bad temper, and, besides, they were pleased to see horrid old Stamp-About stuck up on his own chimney-pot. And will you believe it, there he had to stay till a downpour of rain came and thinned out the glue.

Poor Mr Stamp-About. He was soaked through, and he missed his footing as he climbed down the roof, bounced down the ladder, and landed with a bump on the ground.

"Stamp-About! What *do* you think you are doing, sitting on a chimney-pot, shouting and yelling like that, and then

93

falling off the roof?" cried his sister. "I'm ashamed of you. You can go straight up to bed. I've had enough of you today!"

And you'll hardly believe it, but Stamp-About had had such a lesson that he did go straight up to bed. He never forgot his day on the chimney-pot – and neither did anyone else!